SHARK DETECTIVE!

by Jessica Olien

BALZER + BRAY
An Imprint of HarperCollins Publishers

To Mom and Grammy

ISBN 978-0-06-235714-4

15 16 17 18 19 SCP 10 9 8 7 6 5 4 3 2 1
❖
First Edition

Shark lived alone in a hotel room in the city.

He loved watching detective shows and eating potato chips . . . sometimes too many.

But in the morning he was
still just a lonely shark.

Then one day Shark saw a poster,
and he knew what he had to do.
He would become . . .

To solve the mystery Shark would have to learn to:

look like a kitty · · ·

sniff sniff

sniff like a kitty · · ·

think like a kitty.

He went to the library to research.

He centered himself by doing Tai Chi.

Shark began his investigation by looking for witnesses.

Everywhere he went people screamed and hid.

Shark was beginning to think that he wasn't cut out for detective work. He was getting ready to go home and put on his pajamas when . . .

MEOW!

Shark stood very still.

He listened.

He waited.

Then he had an idea.

MEOW!

The cat's family was so grateful to Shark . . .

. . . that they asked him to stay for good.